A Gift For:

From:

How to Use Your Interactive Storybook & Story Buddy:

1. Press your Story Buddy's ear to start.
2. Read the story aloud in a quiet place. Speak in a clear voice when you see the highlighted phrases.
3. Listen to your buddy respond with several different phrases throughout the book.

Clarity and speed of reading affect Watson's response. He may not always respond to young children.

Watch for even more Interactive Storybooks and Story Buddies. For more information, visit us on the Web at www.Hallmark.com/StoryBuddy.

Copyright © 2011 Hallmark Licensing, Inc.

Published by Hallmark Gift Books,
a division of Hallmark Cards, Inc.,
Kansas City, MO 64141
Visit us on the Web at www.Hallmark.com.

Editors: Emily Osborn and Megan Langford
Art Director: Kevin Swanson
Designer: Mary Eakin
Production Artist: Dan Horton

ISBN: 978-1-59530-356-1
KOB8005
Printed and bound in China
MAR11

— BOOK 1 —

Watson and the Case of The Sneaky Stealer

By **Lisa Riggin** | Illustrated by **Karla Taylor**

Hallmark
GIFT BOOKS

One beautiful spring day, a clever raccoon named
Watson was walking in the woods and wondering
to himself why grass grows up and rain falls down.
He just couldn't help himself— Watson loved
solving mysteries.

All the animals in the forest knew that whenever there was a mystery, Watson was the one to call. That was because Watson had the best sniffer in the woods for nosing out clues!

Watson had just started sniffing at the grass when suddenly there was a loud meowing coming from the bushes. "Watson! Somebody call Watson!"

Watson jumped through a bumbleberry
bush and landed nose to nose with Candy Cat.
"Watson, I could really use your help!"

Candy led Watson to the old oak tree in the clearing. Brushing away a pile of leaves, she uncovered balls of yarn in every color of the rainbow—except one. "Someone has taken my favorite yellow yarn," Candy cried. "I simply have to have it back."

Watson started sniffing for clues right away. He picked up a rock and tickled the worm hanging on underneath.

"Hmmm," thought the clever raccoon. Maybe a woolly worm had needed the yarn to make a sweater. He was just about to tell Candy his theory when a great quacking broke out. "Watson! Somebody call Watson!"

Candy Cat and Watson ran toward the quacking and found David and Darla Duck frantically herding their ducklings together. As soon as Darla saw Watson, she quacked, "Oh, Watson, I could really use your help!"

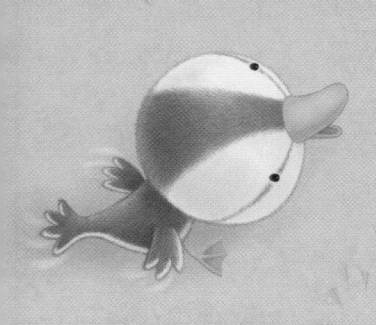

The ducks told **Watson** about the trail
of soft, fuzzy down they had carefully made
for their ducklings to follow to the pond.
When David and Darla checked on the
ducklings, they were waddling in a circle—
someone had taken away half the trail!

Watson set to work sniffing for clues. Shaking off the down that stuck to his tail, he had an idea. Perhaps a horde of hedgehogs made away with the down stuck to their quills. But before he could break the case, he heard some serious squeaking. "Watson! Somebody call Watson!"

The animals rushed toward the squeak and discovered Ronald Rat scurrying back and forth in front of his garden muttering to himself, "It's gone! My rope—it's gone!"

Ronald called Watson over to take a look at the missing section of fence. "Watson, it was one of my greatest treasures!"

Watson began to feel a little overwhelmed.
There sure were a lot of mysteries to solve today,
and he didn't want to disappoint his friends!
    "Can you help me, Watson?" asked the rat.
    "Well," said Watson. "I think so. I mean—"
    "Of course you can!" cried Darla Duck.
"Watson, we believe in you!"

So Watson started looking for clues right away. He sniffed the peas and wondered what kind of creature could have taken the rope, when all of a sudden, Candy Cat mewed, "My yarn! My beautiful yellow yarn!"

And there it was: peeking around the edge of Ronald Rat's pea patch was a bit of yellow yarn. Watson had a brilliant idea.

With Watson in the lead, the group tracked the trail of yellow yarn from Ronald Rat's garden, past the ducks' pond, and through the woods until they found themselves circled around the old oak tree.

"Look," squeaked Ronald. "Watson! It must be up there!"

Slowly, Watson pushed back the leaves, and there in the crook of the branch was a mother bird and four chirping baby birds. "Ooh," whispered the animals when they saw all of their treasures woven into the tiny nest.

Suddenly, it didn't matter if they got their belongings back. They were just happy to be able to help out the tiny birds.

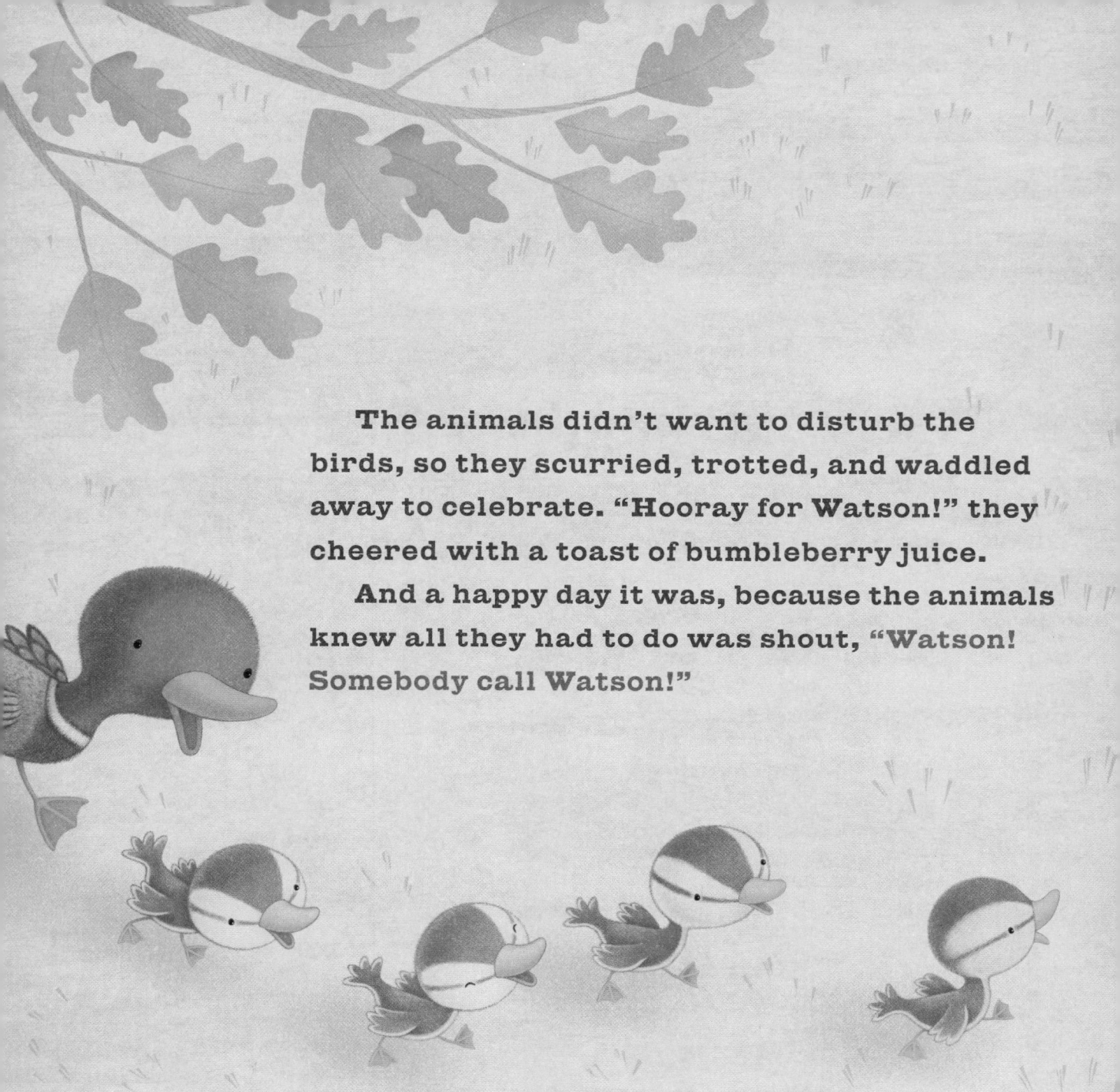

The animals didn't want to disturb the birds, so they scurried, trotted, and waddled away to celebrate. "Hooray for Watson!" they cheered with a toast of bumbleberry juice.

And a happy day it was, because the animals knew all they had to do was shout, "Watson! Somebody call Watson!"

And help would soon be there, because their friend Watson loved solving mysteries!

Did you have fun solving
this mystery with **Watson**?
Tell us about it!

Please send your comments to:
Hallmark Book Feedback
P.O. Box 419034
Mail Drop 215
Kansas City, MO 64141

Or e-mail us at:
booknotes@hallmark.com